The Sorcerer's Apprentice

by Mary Jane Begin

LITTLE, BROWN AND COMPANY

New York ~ Boston

Little, Brown and Company

Time Warner Book Group
1271 Avenue of the Americas, New York, NY 10020
Visit our Web site at www.lb-kids.com

First Edition

Library of Congress Cataloging-in-Publication Data

Begin, Mary Jane.
  The sorcerer's apprentice / written and illustrated by Mary Jane Begin. — 1st ed.
      p. cm.
  Summary: A sorcerer's young apprentice attempts to practice magic in her master's
absence, with disastrous results.
  ISBN 0-316-73611-2
  [1. Fairy tales. 2. Magic--Fiction.] I. Title.
  PZ8.B39So 2005
  [E]—dc22
                                                                      2004025085

10 9 8 7 6 5 4 3 2 1

Book design by Alison Impey

IM

Printed in Singapore

The illustrations for this book were done in acrylic on pastel paper.
The text was set in Perpetua, and the display type is Ovidius.

For my father, for my mother, And for teachers and students everywhere.

 any years ago, when the moon was still young, and everyone still believed in magic, there lived a sorcerer. He could beckon the clouds to speak, coax the trees to dance, and charm the wildest of creatures. He could also guide away evil spirits and heal those that were broken or lost. He was known far and wide for his skills, and he was always willing to share with others what he knew. One day, a mother and her daughter traveled a great distance to ask the sorcerer for the kind of help that only he could give.

As he was also a kind man, the sorcerer offered his guests some dinner and a room for the night. When the meal was finished, he entertained them by making the plates spin in circles and the table walk like a four-legged beast. He then waved his hands and called to the chairs,

With strings, harp, and lute,
Piano and flute,
Perform in this place
With beauty and grace.

The chairs played on into the evening, making music of every kind, until the guests were ready for sleep. But before the sorcerer went off to weave his own dreams, he asked the young girl what she wished for. "I want nothing more than to learn your skills of magic and healing," she told the sorcerer. As the sorcerer was in need of an apprentice, he happily obliged.

$\mathcal{B}$eing an apprentice to a great sorcerer, however, was not exactly what the young girl expected. She washed dishes, swept floors, chopped wood for the fire and carried water from the well. Tirelessly she worked day and night, eagerly waiting to learn a spell or simple charm.

After weeks of hard work, she finally asked the sorcerer, "I mean no disrespect, Master, but why can't you teach me how to wash the dishes with the wave of my hand? Why must I clean and sweep, instead of learning magic?"

The sorcerer looked sternly at the apprentice and said simply, "Some things we must do for ourselves."

The apprentice did not understand. If we must do some things for ourselves, she wondered, then why shouldn't the sorcerer do his own chores? One day, while she was working nearby, she became even more confused when she overheard the sorcerer casting a spell.

Sweep away dust, clean as you must.
Be swift and be neat, until the task is complete.

The broom then sprang to life.

The next day, before the sorcerer left for town, he gave the apprentice the longest list of chores thus far. One task after another she completed, tiring and becoming more careless as the day wore on. The apprentice stumbled wearily as she carried two buckets of water to fill the cauldron, spilling water everywhere.

"I'll never fill that cauldron!" she cried out, on the verge of tears. But then, spotting a broom by the door, she had an idea. Hadn't the sorcerer said that she must learn to do some things for herself? She began to chant:

> *Wander hither across the floor.*
> *Go up the stairs and out the door.*
> *Fetch some water from the well.*
> *Fill the cauldron. Heed my spell!*

For a moment, the apprentice was sure her magic had failed. She had just started to pick up the water buckets when she heard a rustling sound. Suddenly, looming above her was a broom, staring at her. As the girl watched in amazement, it left the kitchen and returned with full buckets, dumping the water into the cauldron.

ack and forth, up and down the stairs the broom swished, again and again. The apprentice rested comfortably until the cauldron was full.

Then, she paused in front of the broom and chanted,

You've done your best,
Now take a rest!
Stand by the door,
As you were before.

But the broom would not stop. It gathered the water faster and faster, filling the cauldron to the brim. The apprentice cried out as the water began to overflow.

Please, please, you must STOP!
The water buckets you must drop!
Your task is through,
And you must do
Whatever I command you!

The apprentice chased the broom up the stairs. She tried desperately to block its path, but the broom knocked her to the ground. When she looked up, the apprentice spied an axe by the wood pile. "NOW YOU'LL STOP!" she shouted as she grabbed the axe and brought it down on the broom. The apprentice chopped it into many bits. The broom was no more.

The exhausted girl wiped her brow. "There is much more work to be done now," she said with a heavy sigh as she bent down to pick up the buckets.

*J*ust then, the apprentice heard a familiar rustling sound. Turning swiftly around, she shrieked. Facing her was an entire army of brooms! Holding buckets full of water, they stared at her with cold, strange eyes. Then they pushed past the cowering girl and marched to the overflowing cauldron.

As the room began to fill with water, the apprentice cried, "Master, MASTER! Help me, please!"

The sorcerer, who was just returning from the village, heard the apprentice cry out, and raced down the stairs. Seeing the chaos, he stretched out his hands toward the brooms and chanted:

Be as it was,
That is my will.
Brooms and water
Shall now all be still.

The water rose high into the air and swirled past the sorcerer, back to the well. The army of brooms disappeared in a cloud of mist. When the apprentice looked around the room, the old broom was back in its place, and everything was as it had been.

As the sorcerer slowly walked down the stairs the apprentice explained quietly, "When you said that some things we must do for ourselves...I thought you meant magic."

The sorcerer looked at the apprentice with smiling eyes, but serious words. "Through hard work and practice, you can learn to have the patience to do anything...and a good sorcerer must be patient above all else." He placed his hand gently on her shoulder. "Do you understand?"

"I think so," answered the apprentice. "But if that is so, why then did *you* use magic to clean the room?"

"Ahhh...," said the sorcerer, understanding her confusion. He answered simply, "The hard work of a sorcerer is not the same as that of an apprentice. Someday, you will understand this more clearly." The apprentice nodded solemnly and with great relief.

And as time passed, her patience and talent as a young apprentice grew, and grew...

ntil
one day,
many years
later, she too became a
sorcerer. It was only then
that she understood exactly
what the sorcerer had meant.